Text by Teresa Heapy
Illustrations by Lucy Fleming
Text and illustrations copyright © 2017 by Bloomsbury Publishing Plc

First published in Great Britain in November 2017 by Bloomsbury Publishing Plc
Published in the United States of America in November 2017
by Bloomsbury Children's Books
www.bloomsbury.com

Bloomsbury is a registered trademark of Bloomsbury Publishing Plc

For information about permission to reproduce selections from this book, write to
Permissions, Bloomsbury Children's Books, 1385 Broadway, New York, New York 10018
Bloomsbury books may be purchased for business or promotional use. For information on bulk purchases please contact
Macmillan Corporate and Premium Sales Department at specialmarkets@macmillan.com

Library of Congress Cataloging-in-Publication Data
available upon request
ISBN 978-1-68119-690-9 (hardcover)
ISBN 978-1-68119-718-0 (e-book) • ISBN 978-1-68119-719-7 (e-PDF)

Typeset in Garden Pro and Emily's Candy
Book design by Maia Fjord
Printed in China by Leo Paper Products, Heshan, Guangdong
2 4 6 8 10 9 7 5 3 1

All papers used by Bloomsbury Publishing, Inc., are natural, recyclable products
made from wood grown in well-managed forests. The manufacturing processes
conform to the environmental regulations of the country of origin.

Princess Snowbelle

Libby Frost

BLOOMSBURY

NEW YORK LONDON OXFORD NEW DELHI SYDNEY

Snowbelle, princess of Frostovia, stood in her turret window looking out at the Opaline Mountains and singing softly to herself. "Sparks, I'm so excited!" she exclaimed. She gave her white cat a stroke. Sparks snuggled up to her.

"But I'm a little bit scared, too," she whispered. "Mother and Father asked me to sing the Opening Song at the Snow Ball tonight, and I've never performed for the whole kingdom!"

Sparks batted Snowbelle's charm bracelet and purred.

"Maybe I'll go and talk to them," she said, and Sparks meowed in agreement.

Princess Snowbelle ran from her room and down the staircase to the grand ballroom in the Opaline Palace.

The ballroom already shimmered and glowed, and beautiful, tinkling music played as her father and mother danced across the marble floor.

"Come and join us!" they called. Snowbelle held her parents' hands, and together, they twirled around the room.

"What's wrong, dearest?" asked her mother. "Are you nervous about singing tonight?"

"A little," admitted Snowbelle. "What if I make a mistake?"

"Don't worry, my princess. We will be there to cheer you on," said her father. "And don't forget you'll have your friend Sparkleshine with you. Friendship is like magic and can help you get through anything."

Snowbelle spun to a stop and kissed her parents. "All right," she said, "I'll practice one more time, and then I'll be ready!"

Snowbelle ran back to
her tower room.
"Now," she said, "all I need is
Sparkleshine! I hope she arrives
soon! She must be on her way
through the forest now . . ."

Snowbelle looked out her turret window . . .

. . . and saw a huge snowstorm swirling over the mountains. So much snow was falling that soon it would be impossible to see anything at all through the waves of white.

"Oh no! Poor Sparkleshine will be stranded!" said Snowbelle. "I must go and find her."

Snowbelle put on her warmest cloak and rushed to the stables.
"Icetail, we must ride out into the snow and find Sparkleshine!"

Icetail tossed her head, whinnied, and stomped. She loved snow.

Together they galloped into the heart of the snowstorm. The snow piled higher than Icetail's hooves, but still they pushed forward. "Sparkleshine!" called Snowbelle. "Where are you?"

Around them the snow whirled and the wind
whistled, until all they could see was white.

"Icetail," said Snowbelle, her teeth chattering from the cold, "I think we're lost!"

"I know," she said. "I can use my charm bracelet to find Sparkleshine. It always helps to have a bit of magic!"

She shook her wrist and the delicate silver snowflake charm tinkled.
"We need light, little charm," whispered Snowbelle. "Light, to help us see!"

All at once, a beautiful glimmering light burst from the snowflake charm. It lit a path through the forest.

"Sparkleshine must be this way!" said Snowbelle. "Come on, Icetail!"

They galloped through the
illuminated forest.
A squirrel bounced into the
glowing path and ran with them.

Next a blackbird joined . . .

. . . and then a family of rabbits.

"Look!" said Snowbelle. "The
animals want to help us!"

Soon they reached a huge tree in the center of the forest.
The squirrel bounded onto a branch, the blackbird flapped
his wings, and the rabbits hopped in circles until Snowbelle saw
Sparkleshine, huddled, shivering against the trunk of the tree.

"Oh, Snowbelle! Thank goodness you're here!" said Sparkleshine. "I got lost and had to find shelter!"

"We got lost, too, but we had a little help!" Snowbelle smiled. "I'm so glad to see you, Sparkleshine. Now let's get back to the palace."

Together, the friends rode through the snowy forest, guided by Snowbelle's light.

When they got to the castle, the snow started to clear and the sky sparkled blue once again.

Snowbelle turned to her new forest friends. "Thank you for your help. I hope you'll stay for the Snow Ball!"

The girls raced up to Snowbelle's room, where beautiful dresses awaited them.

"Oh!" said Sparkleshine. "I'm so very excited!"

"Me too," said Snowbelle, "and only a *little* nervous, now that you're here with me."

"Ready?" whispered Sparkleshine.
"Ready!" Snowbelle smiled.

Holding hands, the two girls walked into the
ballroom to wild applause.

"Welcome to the Snow Ball!" said Princess Snowbelle.
"And now, Sparkleshine and I will perform the
Opening Song!"

"You need never be afraid, On this you can depend:
Even in a whirling snowstorm . . .

"You can always find a friend!"

The crowd cheered, and Snowbelle's heart fluttered with joy.

"Oh, what a perfect Snow Ball!" said Snowbelle. "Friendship and a little bit of magic really did get me through!"

She gently shook her charm bracelet to hear it tinkle. "I can't wait for the next snowy day!"